A PART OF

my quiet times

COLLECTION

www.myquiettimes.com

Wabby Wabbit® is a registered trademark of Kevin Roth/
Star Gazer Productions. All rights reserved.
Copyright 2010, Kevin Roth/My Quiet Times, LLC.
Written by Kevin Roth
Illustrated by Maggie Anthony
Edited by Christopher Fitzpatrick
Cover Design by Laura Vantine
Book Layout by Crysania Weese

Please visit:
www.myquiettimes.com

A PART OF

my quiet times
COLLECTION

Title: The Tales of Wabby - Love Soup
Publisher: My Quiet Times, LLC.

ISBN 978-0-9793393-7-0

The Tales of Wabby
LOVE SOUP

1

On a fine summer morning, the sun rose high in the sky, and the air was sweet with the smell of fresh flowers.

The seeds in Grandma Bunny's garden had grown to be large vines and plants, each one with plump vegetables ready for picking: crunchy carrots, sweet parsnips, and soft leafy greens.

After gently picking the vegetables, Wabby placed them carefully in a large basket near the end of the driveway with a sign that read:

WABBY'S VEGETABLE STAND
A PENNY PER VEGETABLE
THANK YOU
LOVE, WABBY

3

Since the vegetables were ripe and ready,
surely no one could resist buying some for
their supper!

Later that afternoon, Wabby came to see just
how many vegetables had been sold.

To his surprise, not one piece was taken –
no one was going to enjoy his sweet fresh
vegetables with their supper tonight.

Wabby took the big basket of vegetables to Grandma Bunny and complained, "Oh, phooey blooey. Nobody wants any of my vegetables!"

Grandma Bunny smiled and asked, "Do you want to know the secret of how to get everyone to want your vegetables?"

Wabby loved secrets. "Tell me, tell me, tell me," he cried, hopping up on her lap so she could share her big secret.

Holding Wabby close in her arms, she whispered gently in his ear, "When you have an overflowing garden, and so much to give – you just make love soup."

"Love soup? How do you make love soup?" he asked.

"Love soup is made by putting all the food you have in a big pot, and with every stir you think about loving and helping people feel happy and loved all over," she answered.

"But what if they're not hungry?" Wabby asked.

"Once they smell the love coming out of the pot, their tummy's will go yummy, and they will surely be hungry," she said.

Wabby was so very excited!

In the kitchen, Grandma Bunny cut up all of the vegetables into bite-sized chunks. Wabby placed all the pieces inside the big cooking pot.

"Is it love soup yet?" he asked.

"Not yet," she answered gently. "Now we'll add some fresh spring water."

With the pot now half full of water, Wabby looked deep into it and asked again, "Is it love soup yet?"

"Not quite yet," she told him patiently.

Placing a large wooden spoon in Wabby's little paw, Grandma Bunny explained, "Now you must stir the vegetables ever so slowly. With every stir, you must think all about how happy folks will feel when they know that you have made love soup just for them. It will fill their bellies and take away their cares like magic."

So Wabby eagerly stirred the pot, waiting for the magic to appear. But nothing seemed to happen. After a few minutes, he asked, "Is it love soup yet?"

"No, not yet. Keep stirring, Wabby," Grandma Bunny told him.

Wabby stirred and stirred, but all he could think about was how much work it was to stir the big pot of vegetables. "Alright," Wabby said impatiently. "Now it's *got* to be love soup!"

Bringing the spoon up to his mouth for a taste, he gently blew on the broth to cool it down. Then he began to slowly sip his magical love soup.

"Yuck! This doesn't taste good at all!"
Wabby exclaimed.

"Well, I guess you didn't put enough love into it," Grandma Bunny replied. "When you have the right amount of love, it will taste yummy in your tummy."

And so Wabby stirred, stirred, and stirred some more. Making love soup was a lot of work! With Grandma Bunny's help, he poured a little into a bowl and sampled his soup, but it still seemed to taste the same. "This is yucky mucky soup,"
Wabby sighed.

Using the wooden spoon, Grandma Bunny took a taste herself. After a moment, she shook her head from side to side. "Now, Wabby, it's not just how much work you put into making the soup, but what you put *into* the work that makes the difference. Don't forget the most special ingredient – love."

Wabby was very confused. You can love someone, but how do you put love *into* something?

So he did what he always does when he has a big question that needs an answer. Rubbing the little white patch of fur in the shape of a heart, right behind his ear, Wabby asked deep down inside of himself:

How can I put the love *into* my love soup?

And with love and wisdom he heard:

16

Make a little smile, stir it for awhile.
Invite a friend to share, show them that you care.
Say, "Come on over, dude, I've got some loving food!
It's Love Soup for you!"

Love Soup is good for you.
Fills your heart and your belly, too.
Nothing taste better with a friend or two
Than Love Soup for me and you!

Life can be sweeter than apple pie
When you're laughing, and eating,
And you're satisfied.
There's lots of joy in our eyes
When there's Love Soup for you.

Love Soup is good for you
Fills your heart and your belly too.
Nothing tastes better with a friend or two
Than Love Soup for me and you!

And so Wabby stirred, stirred, and stirred. He thought with all of his head and heart about how happy his friends would feel once they tasted all the love in their soup.

Suddenly, he started to smell something wonderful coming out of the pot. Again he took the little wooden spoon for a taste. It was the most scrumptious soup he'd ever had! "It's love soup! It's love soup!" he exclaimed, hopping up and down with joy.

Grandma Bunny took a little taste – but this time she nodded her head up and down. "Oh little Wabby, now you can taste the love!" she said kissing him on his furry little nose. "Now, you must add the last and most important secret ingredient of all."

Wabby scratched his head. "What's that Grandma Bunny? Isn't it love soup already?"

"It's not really love soup until you share it with friends that you love," she told him.

"Oh, yes," Wabby said. "I almost forgot. That's when love soup tastes its best!"

That evening, Wabby gathered some of his friends together at Grandma Bunny's table.

23

Each one brought laughter, music, and stories to tell. Before they knew it, every drop of Wabby's love soup had been eaten. With their bellies and their hearts full, they thanked him for the splendid meal he had prepared.

Oh, how they loved their Wabby.

With the last guest gone, the table was cleared, and all the dishes were washed and put away.

As Grandma Bunny settled Wabby into bed, he said, "We must never, ever forget how to make Love Soup. First, the vegetables, then the water, then stir, stir, stir – and then the LOVE! I'm glad you gave me the love Grandma Bunny!"

As he rubbed his full little belly, Wabby let out a very loud belch. With embarrassment, he quickly covered his mouth with his little paw, as polite rabbits should do. "'Cuse me!" he said with a grin.

Grandma Bunny giggled, "Goodness, there certainly is a lot of love inside of you! You're a very lucky rabbit."

She kissed him gently on his furry little nose and said, "Don't forget I love you," as she tucked him into bed and played him his favorite lullaby.

THE END

About the Author

Kevin Roth is an award winning singer, songwriter, author, and performer. Known internationally as one of the world's most innovative dulcimer players and singers, his early recordings on Folkways Records are now part of The Smithsonian Folkways Collection. His voice has been heard around the world as the singer of the hit PBS children's television show, *Shining Time Station*, based on Thomas the Tank Engine.

In 2010, *The Tales of Wabby* was released as part of an original series of books and music featuring the original character, Wabby Wabbit. Wabby teaches children to make decisions about their lives by listening to their heart with love and wisdom.

His new line of books and music can be found as part of the *My Quiet Times* brand line.

About the Artist

Maggie Anthony was born and raised in Poland, where she worked as a film animator, background and sketch artist. Since she came to United States in 2002, she expanded her talents to include personal portraits, book illustration, and decorative painting. Maggie is part of the creative team for *The Tales of Wabb*y which she utterly enjoys.